D1297781

My

Sound Box

by Jane Belk Moncure

illustrated by Linda Sommers

THE CHILD'S WORLD

MANKATO, MN 56001

Library of Congress Cataloging in Publication Data

Moncure, Jane Belk.
  My k sound box.

  (Sound box books)
  SUMMARY: A little boy fills his sound box
with many words beginning with the letter "k".
  [1. Alphabet] I. Sommers, Linda.
PZ7.M739Myk   [E]   78-22034
ISBN 0-89565-050-9 -1991 Edition

My "k" Sound Box

Little k had a box.

"I will find things that begin with my 'k' sound," he said.

"I will put them into my sound  box.

But first, I will be a king."

So he dressed up as a king.

Then Little  went for a walk.

He found a koala.

Did he put the koala into his box?

box

He did.

Next, Little  found

kingbirds.

Did he put the kingbirds
into his box?
He did.

Then Little  found a kitty.

"Kitty, kitty," he called.

Lots and lots of kittens came . . .

from everywhere!

Little [crown] tried to put the kittens into the box. But the kingbirds did not like that!

Do you know why?
What could Little do?   He found a . . .

15

kangaroo.

The kangaroo had a big pocket.

Little  put all the kittens into the pocket.

"A king can do anything!" said Little

So he played the   kettledrum.
Then he put it into the box.

Next, he looked through a kaleidoscope.
Here is what he saw.

He put the kaleidoscope into the box too.

Then Little  found kites,

lots and lots of kites.

"I will fly a kite," he said.

But the wind blew the kite away.
The kingbirds flew after the kite.

The kittens kicked the kangaroo.

kerchoo!

The kangaroo sneezed, "Kerchoo!"
and blew . . .

everything into a

kindergarten.

kites

kittens

kingbird

kettledrum

koala

kitter

26

My, what fun the children had!

kangaroo

kaleidoscope

kingbird

kitten

kitten

Can you read these words with Little ?

kiss

keg

katydid

ketchup

kettle

key

kitchen

kid

kid

kayak

kimono

29

About the Author

Jane Belk Moncure, author of many books and stories for young children, is a graduate of Virginia Commonwealth University and Columbia University. She has taught nursery, kindergarten and primary children in Europe and America. Mrs. Moncure has taught early childhood education while serving on the faculties of Virginia Commonwealth University and the University of Richmond. She was the first president of the Virginia Association for Early Childhood Education and has been recognized widely for her services to young children. She is married to Dr. James A. Moncure, Vice President of Elon College, and currently teaches in Burlington, North Carolina.